TOY WORDS

Jenny Tyler
Illustrated by Sue Stitt

With consultant advice from John Newson and Gillian Hartley of the Child Development Research Unit at Nottingham University, and Robyn Gee.

Designed by Kim Blundell and Mary Cartwright

bricks

train

car

doll

tractor

aeroplane

ball

telephone

puzzle

balloon

telephone

train

ball

puzzle

balloon

doll

aeroplane

car

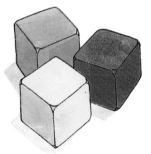

bricks

tractor